This book unfortunately belongs to:

_____

This book is dedicated to all of the characters and authors who thought their book was the worst book in the whole entire world. It can't get much worse than this.

You're welcome.

www.ackersbooks.com

Entire World Books: 1

All elaborate and masterful illustrations and words produced by Joey Acker. All rights reserved. That means don't copy, like you could, anything from this book. Because I know you want to...

Copyright Joey and Melanie Acker 2019

Melanie chose to excuse herself from this book. That was probably a good idea...

ISBN-13: 978-1-7327456-9-8

The WORST Book

in the Whole Entire World

Joey Acker

Congratulations.

You are now reading the worst book in the whole entire world.

I bet you are wondering why this is the worst book in the whole entire world.

Are you sitting down?

Because you are about to find out why this book is the worst.

Reason #1: there is only one sentence on every page.

Except for that page.

And that one. Awkward.

Reason #2: remember that super awesome red balloon on the cover?

It blew away.

Reason #3: there are GROSS words in this book!

Booger

Stinky

Toot

Booty

Booger Booty

Stinky Booty

Toot Booty

Ohhhhhhhhhh no! Now I remember!

Just don't turn the next page.

Seriously.

Put this book down and walk away.

I'm leaving.

Booger toot

Stinky toot

Toot **booger**

Stinky booger

Toot **booger** stinky **booty**

I told you NOT to turn the page.

Must we go on?

Are you absolutely, positively, most indefinitely sure you want to keep reading this horrible, horrible book?

You chose poorly.

At least I warned you.

Reason #4: I am all alone.

I am the only person, place, or thing in this book.

That's called a ...

NOUN

That's just great.

Reason #5: this book is educational.

Is this book the worst or what?

Reason #6: you're not alone!

Reason #7: this book is NOT funny.

Hahahahahaha!

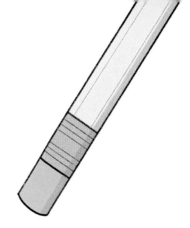

Wait. What's that?

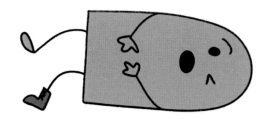

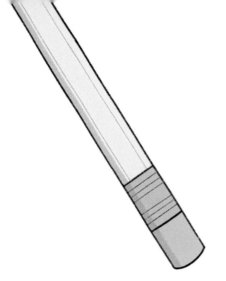

Noooooooo!

Bye bye, booger booty.

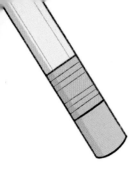

Maybe this isn't the worst book in the whole entire world.

Reason #8: the end.